ALLUMETTE

A fable, with due respect to
Hans Christian Andersen, the Grimm Brothers,
and the Honorable Ambrose Bierce

By Tomi Ungerer

Parents' Magazine Press • New York

Library of Congress Cataloging in Publication Data
Ungerer, Tomi, 1931-
   Allumette.
   SUMMARY: Granted her wishes for all the good things
she never had, an impoverished orphan is so deluged with
commodities that she opens a headquarters for distrib-
uting them to the world's poor.
   [1. Fairy.tales.   2. Orphans—Fiction]   I. Title.
PZ8.U84A   [E]   73-23055
ISBN 0-8193-0730-0   ISBN 0-8193-0731-9 (lib. bdg.)

J-4

A 66577
My~

Summer and winter, spring and fall,
Allumette dressed in rags.
She had no home. She had no parents.

Allumette fed on scraps from garbage bins,
found shelter in empty doorways
and slept in abandoned cars.
She eked out a living, wandering the city,
selling matches nobody wanted.
"Look at that kid!" someone would say.
"Why isn't she selling flowers—or even lighters?
But matches!!! Who needs matches!"

Winter was here. Christmas had come to town.
Streets festooned with garlands and cardboard angels
were lively with people buying and selling presents.
The air was vibrant with organ music.
Costumed Santas were pealing bells.
Warm, in furs and woolens,
too happy to notice poor Allumette,
the crowds scurried by.

It was late now, and the streets were empty. Famished, fatigued, feet frozen, Allumette stopped in front of a pastry shop. She pressed her little nose against the glass to savor the cakes on display.

BUT NOT FOR LONG...

Out rushed the baker, Monsieur Lacroute, in a torrent of foul insults: "Off with you, varmint, smudging my window front, drooling on my sidewalk!

Scram, scum, or I shall flatten you with my rolling pin."

Terrified, the poor little girl ran off, head over heels into the darkness.

Allumette reached a building site.
There, with her last match, she lit a fire.
Up it flared, bright and hot. The heat felt good.
BUT NOT FOR LONG...

The silence was suddenly shattered by howls of
sirens. A pack of firetrucks would soon rush
into the lot. Allumette was on the run again,
her thin shadow dissolving into the night.

Half-starved, Allumette didn't get very far.
Her strength was giving out,
and her scrawny little body was giving up.
Out of breath, shaking, too weak even to walk,
she collapsed on the pavement.
"Oh what," Allumette thought, "if this is the end?"
And she started to pray as hard as she could:
"Please let me live a little bit more, long
enough to have a taste of cake, or just one
slice of turkey, or ham.
Oh how I wish—somebody listen,
please listen to me."
It was midnight and belfries were chiming
when a flash and a sudden clap of thunder
jarred Allumette out of her frozen daze.

A split second later,
a monumental birthday cake crashed at her feet.
Dumbfounded, she was picking crumbs off the pavement
when a flock of roasted turkeys came
whizzing down.
A hoard of hams followed suit.

Mohair blankets and a purple coverlet came flopping
down and wrapped themselves around her shoulders.
Somebody *had* been listening. Allumette's wishes
were coming true. Links of sausage dropped in a ring
around her, audience-like. A tricycle landed at her feet.
Then there was a lull. BUT NOT FOR LONG...
A second flash of lightning and—Bang!
The wishing spell burst with renewed vigor.

Heavy clumps of clouds unloaded the wildest array
of things imaginable. Everything, *everything* Allumette
had ever wished for came pouring down.

The ground trembled, street lamps quivered under the
impact. The baker and his wife were still awake, counting
money. Startled by the thunder and the crashing outside,
Monsieur Lacroute peeked through the shutter.
"Incroyable!" he exclaimed. "It's pouring all sorts of stuff."
They rushed out green with greed
to snatch some of the precious goods, and were
caught in a deluge of plumbing equipment.
Their screams were muffled at once by
huge blobs of strawberry jelly.

The skies cleared at dawn. By then, merchandise
had piled up to a height of 37 feet.
Allumette came through without a scratch.
"Some wishing that was!" she exclaimed.
Just then, speeding along on his bicycle,
a mailman appeared. His wheels skidded
in a pool of marmalade and he slithered into
the open arms of a life-sized teddy bear.
"Help, don't bite me!" screamed the mailman.

"It's only a teddy bear," explained Allumette
as she helped the victim to his feet.
"Sacre-coeur, it must have run away from the zoo!
What goes on around here anyway? What is all this?"
"All this is mine!" said Allumette.
"I wished for it and it came down last night.
That's all."
"That is *not* all. What are you going to do with it?"
"Give it away. Now. Before things spoil," replied Allumette.
"In that case I'd better get going and tell everyone about it."
Said and done.

Out of hiding they came,
the maimed, the lame,
the hungry and cold,
the young, the old,
the jobless, the joyless,
the sick and the blind
and the weak of mind.
They all emerged
out of their dark, forgotten neighborhoods.
Within their mansions, ill at ease,
feeling cheap and selfish,
the rich watched the endless procession.

"It is a disgrace to the good name of our city,"
shouted the mayor, "this repulsive parade of people
who forget where they belong!"
He called for an immediate meeting of the town elders.
They assembled and took measures.
A delegation headed by the mayor would investigate
the scene of turmoil. Riot squads were alerted
and the army was bugled out of its barracks.

In the meantime,
the baker and his wife, bruised blue,
came to Allumette and fell on their knees.
"Little one, whoever you are, forgive us.
We were cruel, let us make it up, accept our help."
Allumette smiled and said:
"Help is exactly what is needed."
Together, they channeled the crowds into
patient lines and started sorting the goods
in a warehouse nearby which belonged to
Monsieur Lacroute.

The mayor was flabbergasted to discover a pale
little girl at the source of the ferment.
Just a child, allotting an endless supply of
gifts to a well-behaved crowd.
The mayor felt embarrassed.
The armed forces felt useless.
For the sake of his popularity,
the mayor scrambled on top of the pile
to make a speech. No one cared,
so after a while he stopped talking.

By now, other volunteers had joined the crowd.
Some wealthy people were moved
to contribute gifts of their own.
Instead of shrinking, the pile kept on growing.
So did the number of poor who were now
streaming in from faraway places.
For good news travels fast. It traveled even faster
when newspapers and magazines got hold of
the story and spread it like butter on hot toast.
Pictures were taken, articles written.

Yet no satisfactory explanation was ever found.
A miracle? Why not.
A flying cornucopia circling the earth,
disgorging itself every thousand years?
Possibly. (Some claimed they saw it.)
A stunt staged by the mayor to get votes
for himself? Could be.
Most children thought it was Santa Claus.
The *real* one. As for Allumette?
She was not interested in explanations.
"All that counts," she would say, "is the good
that came of it."

The baker's warehouse became a beehive of goodwill.
It grew and grew.
Contributions flowed in from all over the world,
and help was sent out in every direction.
Wherever famine, fire, flood or war broke out,
there were some of Allumette's willing volunteers,
doing their best.

There never was another such storm.
Anyway, Allumette, growing up at the head
of her own Matchless Light of the World Foundation,
never made another wish.
She was completely happy and would ask for no more.
Yet on stormy days, when most people take cover,
she runs out on her terrace
and waves at the heavy clumps of clouds rolling by.